Ladybird
Ladybird

Ladybird Ladybird

Vivian French

illustrated by
Selina Young

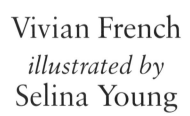

Orion
Children's Books

Ladybird, Ladybird was originally published in Great Britain in 2001
by Orion Children's Books
This new Early Reader edition was first published in 2015
by Orion Children's Books
a division of the Orion Publishing Group Ltd
Orion House
5 Upper St Martin's Lane
London WC2H 9EA
An Hachette UK Company

1 3 5 7 9 10 8 6 4 2

A catalogue record for this book is available
from the British Library

Printed and bound in China

ISBN 978 1 4440 1379 5

for Alfred Sage . s.y

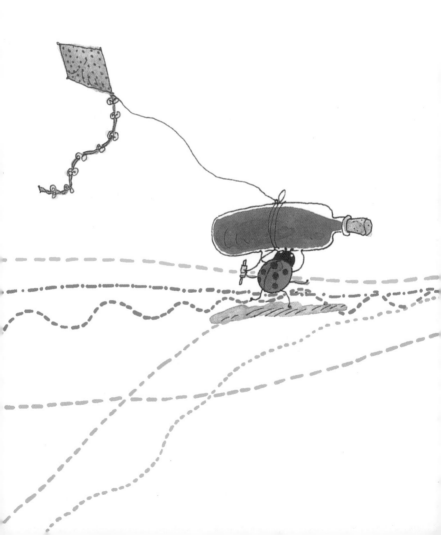

This is Little Ladybird.

And these are his brothers
and sisters.

This is his
big sister, Sue.

This is his brother, Harry.

This is Harry's twin, Alice.

And this is his big brother, Bill.

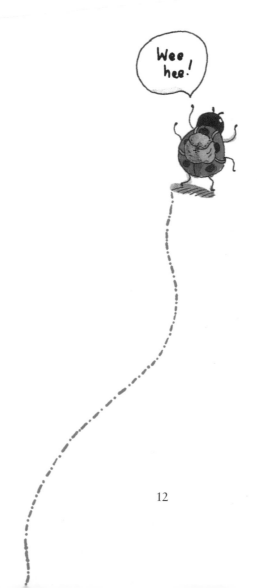

Mrs Ladybird was going
shopping.

First she made breakfast for
her five little ladybirds, and then
she made a list.

"We need milk," she said.
"What else do we need?"

"Butter," said Bill.
"Buns," said Sue.

"Jam!" said Harry.
"Lots and lots of jam!" said Alice.

Little Ladybird came running down the stairs. "What about a yummy iced cake?"

"Not today, dear," said Mrs Ladybird.

Mrs Ladybird picked up the list, and her umbrella, and her shopping trolley.

Then she set out for the shops . . .

hills   shops

home

"Look!" said Little Ladybird.
"Mum's forgotten her purse!"

And he picked up the pink
spotty purse and ran after
Mrs Ladybird.

Mrs Ladybird went past
Auntie June's toadstool house,
but she didn't stop to say hello.

She was in too much of a
hurry to get to the shops . . .

And Little Ladybird hurried
after her.

"Mum! Mum! Look what
I've got!"

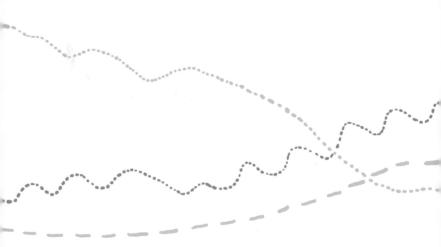

But Mrs Ladybird didn't hear
him, and she didn't stop.

Big sister Sue ran after Little
Ladybird.

But Little Ladybird didn't
hear her. He went on running,
so Sue ran after him.

You arE
nearly at
the Shops

Mrs Ladybird went
hurrying past Uncle Jim's
house.

Uncle Jim came out to
wave, but Mrs Ladybird
didn't stop.

She went hurrying past
Grandma's house. Grandma
was hanging out her washing.

"Hello!" she called, and she
waved a blue hanky, but Mrs
Ladybird didn't wave back.

She was in too much of a
hurry to get to the shops.

Little Ladybird hurried after
Mrs Ladybird, and Sue hurried
after Little Ladybird.

Harry saw his big sister
running after Little Ladybird.
He didn't want to be left
behind. "Sue!" he called, "Sue!"

But big sister Sue didn't
hear him and neither did
Little Ladybird.

They both went on running,
so Harry ran after them.

Mrs Ladybird pattered over the bridge that led to the town.

Spotty and Dotty were fishing in the river, but she didn't stop to watch.

She was in too much of a hurry to get to the shops.

shops

river

good fishing spot

Alice was playing with her kite when she saw Harry running after Sue.

"Wait, Harry, wait!" she shouted.

But Harry didn't hear her,
and nor did Sue, and nor did
Little Ladybird.

They all went on running,
so Alice ran after them.

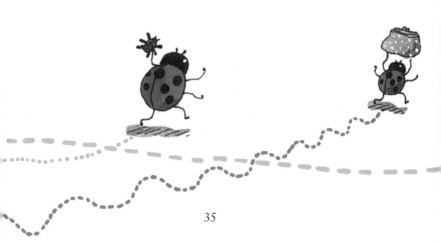

Mrs Ladybird hurried into town. "Where's the Food Hall?"

"Oh! There it is!" And she dashed through the door.

Little Ladybird hurried after her.

"Mum! Mum! Look what I've got!"

Wait Ladybirds please come back!

Sue hurried after Little Ladybird.

Harry hurried after Sue.

Alice hurried after Harry.

And behind them all ran their big brother, Bill.

But nobody heard him, and nobody stopped.

Mrs Ladybird took out her
list.

"I need biscuits, butter, bread
and jam," she said. "Berry jam
would be nice."

And she filled up her
shopping basket, and went
to pay . . .

Berry
Jam

But she had forgotten her
purse!

The five little ladybirds came
running into the Food Hall.

"Here it is, Mummy!"
shouted Little Ladybird.
"Here's your purse!"

Mrs Ladybird picked up Little Ladybird and gave him a great big hug.

"What a wonderful Little Ladybird you are!" she said.

"And I came too," said big sister Sue.

"We all did!" said Alice and Harry and big brother Bill.

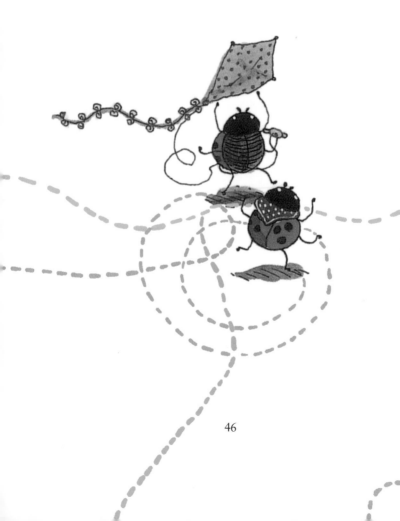

"You're all wonderful," Mrs Ladybird told them. "I think you should have a treat!"

"Can we have a yummy iced cake?" asked Little Ladybird.

Mrs Ladybird nodded.

"We'll buy an extra yummy iced cake."

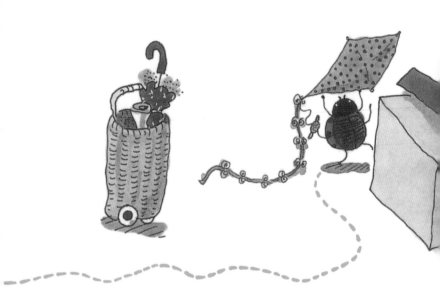

"Hurrah," said Bill and Harry,
and they rushed to find one.

extra
yummy
iced cake

The five little ladybirds helped
carry the shopping home.

Big brother Bill carried
the extra yummy iced cake
very carefully!

They all had a lovely tea.

Alice had one slice of the extra yummy iced cake.

Bill, Harry and Sue had two slices . . .

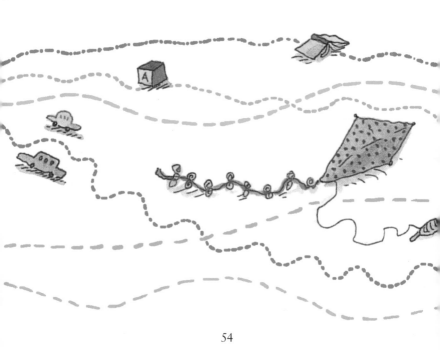

And Little Ladybird had three slices!

"That was the best cake ever," he said.

"Time for bed," said Mrs
Ladybird. "It's been a busy day."

She tucked the five little ladybirds in, and kissed them goodnight.

"Sleep well, my darlings."

But nobody answered.

All five little ladybirds were fast asleep, dreaming of yummy iced cake.

What are you going to read next?

Have more adventures with Horrid Henry,

or save the day with Anthony Ant!

Become a superhero with Monstar,

float off to sea with Algy,

or have your very own Pirates' Picnic.

Grow carrots with

Lottie and Dottie,

make magic with
The Witch Dog,

and cast a
spell with

The Three
Little Magicians.

Enjoy all the Early Readers.

the

orion star